# Touch the Sky Summer

# Touch the Sky Summer

## Jean Van Leeuwen

*pictures by* Dan Andreasen

*Dial Books for Young Readers*  *New York*

Published by Dial Books for Young Readers

A Division of Penguin Books USA Inc.

375 Hudson Street

New York, New York 10014


Text copyright © 1997 by Jean Van Leeuwen

Pictures copyright © 1997 by Dan Andreasen

All rights reserved

Designed by Amelia Lau Carling

Printed in Hong Kong

First Edition

1 3 5 7 9 10 8 6 4 2


Library of Congress Cataloging in Publication Data

Van Leeuwen, Jean.

Touch the sky summer/by Jean Van Leeuwen; pictures by Dan Andreasen.

– 1st ed.   p.   cm.

Summary: Luke and his family take their annual trip to their grandparents'

lakeside cabin where they spend time fishing, camping, and hiking.

ISBN 0-8037-1819-5 (trade).— ISBN 0-8037-1820-9 (lib.)

[1. Vacations—Fiction. 2. Summer—Fiction. 3. Grandparents—

Fiction.] I. Andreasen, Dan, ill. II. Title.

PZ7.V3273Wh 1997 [Fic]—dc20   96-2380   CIP   AC


*The artwork was prepared using oil paints on gesso-primed board.*

*It was then color-separated and reproduced in red, yellow, blue, and black halftones.*

*To Grandma and Grandpa*
*and all the family in the cottage at Silver Bay.*
*And to the memory of Bill Parkinson.*
*J.V.L.*

*For my parents, with warm memories of Hess Lake.*
*D.A.*

We drove and we drove and we drove.

"Are we almost to Grandma and Grandpa's house?" I asked.

"Not yet," said Dad.

Out the window there was nothing to see but cars streaming by, like fish swimming. So we played "I Took a Trip to Grandmother's House and in My Trunk I Packed" and counted license plates and sang "Old MacDonald" until we ran out of animals.

"He kicked me," complained Peter.

"His foot was on my side," I said.

"Let's have lunch," said Mom.

The road got smaller. Up it climbed. Over a mountain, scraping the sky, and down.

"I see it!" cried Peter.

And there was the lake, ringed by mountains and dotted with islands, shining silver in the sun.

The road turned to dirt. We bumped along until it ended at a tiny cabin held in the giant arms of pine trees.

"It looks just the same," sighed Mom.

Then the cabin door opened, and we were gathered in.

I woke up early in a strange place. Why was I sleeping up in the air? Then I remembered, and climbed down from my bunk to see the morning.

Grandpa was already awake. The two of us had breakfast, the crunch of cereal and the twitter of birds the only sounds.

"Shall we go for a walk?" he whispered.

Up the hill we climbed, to the clearing where Grandpa had his garden. He pulled weeds while I picked tomatoes and green beans, long and skinny as fingers, for supper. On we went, to the post office to mail a letter and the general store for milk. Then back beside the lake.

I stood on the end of the dock, peering into the dark water for fish.

"This year you will catch one," said Grandpa.

When we got back, Mom and Dad and Peter were having breakfast.

"Everything is just the same," I told them.

Wait till you see the surprise," I said to Grandma at lunch.
Mom gave me a look. Peter kicked me under the table.

"What surprise?" asked Grandpa.

But I wouldn't say another word.

After lunch Peter and I found the basket of beach toys and we all walked down the narrow path to the lake.

"I can't wait to get in that water," said Mom.

The surprise was bursting to get out. I looked at Peter, and we couldn't help it. We both grinned.

"Ready. Set. Go!" We ran in and started swimming to Mom.

"Well, will you look at that," I heard Grandpa say.

I swam back to shore.

"We know how to swim," I said. "We took lessons."

Grandma wrapped me up warm in her giant beach towel.

"What a super surprise!" she said.

We hiked up Tongue Mountain. It got its name, Dad said, because it looked like a tongue sticking out in the lake.

"We are hunters," said Peter. "Shhh! Don't make a sound."

But I stepped—*crack*—on a stick.

"Now that bear got away," said Peter, frowning.

I looked over my shoulder. There could be bears in these woods. Quickly I ran to catch up to Mom and Dad.

The trail grew steeper. My legs got tired.

"Hang on, buddy," said Dad. "We're almost there."

"I'm going to be first!" shouted Peter, running ahead.

Dad swung me onto his shoulders. "We'll see about that!"

We crashed through the woods like an angry bear. Up another steep place, past a giant rock, past Peter. And suddenly we came out of the trees into blue sky.

"We did it!" I cried.

Resting, we looked down on our big lake grown small. I saw our bay, a red rooftop, a tiny curl of smoke rising from the trees.

"It's our house," I said.

And in case Grandma and Grandpa were looking, I waved.

It can't be raining," said Peter. "Today I am swimming to the raft."

"And I'm going fishing," I said.

But it was.

"There is nothing to do on a rainy day," complained Peter.

"Nonsense," said Grandpa. He built a fire, and Grandma brought out the games. We played dominoes and Chinese checkers and Go Fish. I drew a picture of the giant fish I was going to catch.

After lunch it was still raining. And thundering and lightning.

"How about a jigsaw puzzle?" asked Grandma.

Just then the lights went out.

"Oh no," said Peter. "Now there's really nothing to do."

But Grandpa lit a kerosene lamp. Grandma found some popping corn. She showed us how to shake it in a wire basket over the fire.

"In the old days," said Grandpa, "all we had here were kerosene lamps."

We sat by the fire and ate popcorn and listened to Grandpa tell about the old days, the rain *drip-dripping* on the roof.

It was a nice rainy day.

I stood perfectly still on the end of the dock, waiting for a fish to bite.

Nothing happened.

I watched Peter practicing his swimming with Dad.

Still nothing happened.

Now Peter was throwing a round white rock and diving after it.

Still no nibbles.

Lying on the dock, I peered into the shadowy water. Somewhere down there lived a grandfather fish. We saw him last year.

"Luke!" Peter was waving at me. "I did it! I swam to the raft!"

"Shhh!" I scowled at him. "You're scaring the fish."

I put on a new worm and moved to a new spot.

But nothing happened.

"They bite better out a ways," said someone behind me. It was Mr. Parkinson from down the road. "I'm going out in my boat tomorrow morning. Want to come?"

"Yes!" I said.

It was still dark when I tiptoed out of the cabin, past gray sleeping trees, down to the dock. And there was Mr. Parkinson waiting for me.

Fog hung over the lake like a fallen cloud. We were inside of it. All I could see was mist and all I could hear was the dip of oars. Then Mr. Parkinson stopped rowing.

"Here we are," he said. "My favorite spot."

We baited our hooks.

"The granddaddy of all fish used to live under those rocks," Mr. Parkinson told me. "For years I tried to catch him. Finally I did. And do you know, he jumped out of the water, gave me a dirty look, and just spit out that hook."

"Then what happened?"

"He swam away. I never saw him again."

I dropped in my line. I sat still, hardly breathing, waiting. Nothing happened.

Behind me I heard a splash. But it was only a duck family with three, four, five babies swimming by.

Then I felt the tiniest tug on my line.

"I've got one," I whispered. But just as fast, it was gone.

Silently we sat and watched the night turn into day.

The sun was just peeping over the mountain when I felt another nibble. This one was real.

"Bring him in slow and easy," Mr. Parkinson told me.

I reeled and reeled. The fish pulled. It didn't want to be caught.

"A little more," said Mr. Parkinson.

It was a big one, I could tell. Maybe a grandfather.

"That's it. You've got him now!"

My fish flopped into the boat. It was the biggest I ever caught. Not quite a grandfather, but an uncle at least.

"What a beauty!" said Mr. Parkinson, holding it up.

Then he had a bite and I had another. By the time the sun had climbed into the sky, our pail was full.

I took one oar as we rowed back to shore. And there was Grandpa waiting for me.

"I caught five sunnies!" I told him.

Grandpa cleaned them and Mom cooked them, and we had a fish feast for breakfast.

Please can we camp out?" begged Peter. "Please, please!"

"Okay," said Dad.

So we said good night and went out to sleep in our blanket tent.

The ground was hard. The dark seemed too dark. I couldn't sleep.

"What was that noise?" I whispered.

"I don't hear anything," said Peter, yawning.

The noise came again. I knew it was something. Something big.

"Maybe it's an owl," said Peter.

Maybe it was a bear. What if a bear walked right into our tent?

It came closer. A stick snapped. *Crack!* My heart was thumping like a bass drum. Peter clicked on his flashlight.

Eyes. That was all I saw. A hundred glowing yellow eyes.

And another giant one moving toward us.

"Look at those rascally raccoons trying to get into the garbage can," whispered Dad. He set down his lantern.

Together we watched until the raccoons went away. Then Dad crawled into our tent. His feet stuck out, but he didn't mind. We told jokes and asked each other riddles and Dad told us a creepy ghost story.

After that the three of us curled up like bears and went to sleep.

It was our last day. Peter and I were building a sand fort while everyone else sat talking in chairs.

"It's hot," said Mom. She went in the water. Then Grandpa. Then Dad.

"Can I swim to the raft with you?" asked Peter. And he went too.

I was all alone with Grandma. I dumped a pail of wet sand. I built the walls higher, watching the raft bob in the blue water.

Suddenly I called to Mom, "I'm coming out!"

I paddled and paddled. But the raft seemed so far away.

Mom came to meet me. "A little farther," she said. "A little farther."

My nose was full of water. My arms were like spaghetti. Still I kept paddling.

"Come on, Luke!" called Peter. "You can do it."

Paddle, paddle. I would never get there. Paddle, paddle.

And suddenly there was the raft in front of me.

"You did it!" cried Dad and Peter, pulling me up.

Standing on the raft, I felt tall enough to touch the sky. Grandma on shore seemed so far away. She was waving and clapping. I waved back.

"Come on out!" I called.

Later on we had a picnic on the beach.

Dad built a fire and we had hamburgers and hot dogs and Grandma's best potato salad and slices of dripping pink watermelon for dessert. And marshmallows toasted over the fire on sticks.

Afterward we played catch and looked for the grandfather fish under the dock. Grandpa showed us how to skip stones.

*Plunk, plunk, plunk, plunk* went his stone, making ripples on the silvery water like fat raindrops.

*Plunk, plunk* went Peter's.

*Plunk* went mine.

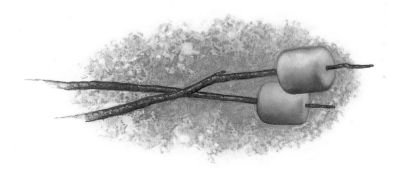

When it got dark we lay on blankets, looking up at the starry sky. "Look," whispered Mom. "A shooting star. Did you see it?"

I saw it. I squeezed my eyes shut and made a wish.
Can you guess what I wished for?